GILDEN-FIRE

Revelstone met the eyes of the invaders
with a wonder such as they had never known.

GILDEN-FIRE

Stephen Donaldson

Illustrations by Peter Goodfellow

COLLINS
London
1983

First published in hardcover in Great Britain
in 1983 by William Collins Sons & Co. Ltd, Glasgow

Copyright © 1981 by Stephen Donaldson
Illustrations copyright © 1983 by Peter Goodfellow

ISBN 0 00 222762 2

Photoset in Linotron Baskerville by
Rowland Phototypesetting Ltd, Bury St Edmunds, Suffolk
Printed in Great Britain by
St Edmundsbury Press, Bury St Edmunds, Suffolk

ILLUSTRATIONS

FOREWORD

GILDEN-FIRE is, in essence, an 'out-take' from THE ILLEARTH WAR. For that reason, it is not a complete story. Rather, it describes an episode which occurred to Korik of the Bloodguard and his mission to Seareach during the early days of THE ILLEARTH WAR, after Thomas Covenant's summoning to the Land but before the commencement of the actual war. This material survived through two drafts of the manuscript, but is entirely absent from the published version of the book.

On that basis, I think it requires some explanation. As a general rule, I use my out-takes for wastepaper. But I've made an exception in this case for a variety of reasons.

Some of them have to do with why GILDEN-FIRE was taken out of THE ILLEARTH WAR in the first place. The version of the manuscript which originally crossed the desk of Lester del Rey at

Ballantine Books was 916 pages long – roughly 261,000 words. That was manifestly too long. With much regret, Lester gave me to understand that I would have to cut 250 pages.

Well, I'm a notorious over-writer; and I was able to eliminate 100 pages simply by squeezing the prose with more than my usual ruthlessness. But after that I had to make a more difficult decision.

As it happened, the original version of THE ILLEARTH WAR was organized in four parts rather than the present three. Part II in that version dealt exclusively with Korik's mission to Seareach; and it eventually provided me with the 150 pages of cuts I still needed. Not because I considered the material to be of secondary importance (I have little sympathy for anyone who considers the fate of the Unhomed, the fidelity of the Bloodguard, and the valour of the Lords to be of secondary importance). On the contrary, I was quite fond of that whole section. No, I put my axe to the roots of my former Part II for reasons of narrative logic.

From the beginning, that section had been

a risky piece of writing. In it, I had used Korik as my viewpoint character. For the first time in the trilogy, I had stepped fully away from Thomas Covenant (or any direct link to the 'real' world). And that proved to be a mistake. It was crucial to the presentation of Covenant's character that he had some good reasons for doubting the substantial 'reality' of the Land. But all his reasons were undercut when I employed someone like Korik – a character with no bond, however oblique, to Covenant's world – for a narrative centre. (THE ILLEARTH WAR does contain two chapters from Lord Mhoram's point of view. But in both cases Mhoram is constantly in the company of either Covenant or Hile Troy. Korik's mission lacked even that connection to the central assumptions on which LORD FOUL'S BANE and THE ILLEARTH WAR were based.) In using Korik as I had, I had informed the reader that the people of the Land were in fact 'real': I had unintentionally denied the logic of Covenant's Unbelief. Which was already too fragile for its own good.

Therefore I took the absolutely essential

[9]

sections of that Part II and recast them as reports which Runnik and Tull brought back to Covenant and Troy – thus preserving the integrity of the narrative perspective from which the story was being viewed. And in the process, I achieved the 150 pages of cuts I needed.

But all of GILDEN-FIRE was lost.

That does not exactly constitute high tragedy. Cutting is part of writing; and narrative logic is more important than authorial fondness. My point is simply that GILDEN-FIRE was cut, not because it was bad, but because it didn't fit well enough.

However, the question remains: if this material didn't fit THE ILLEARTH WAR, why am I inflicting it upon the world now?

The main reason, I suppose, is my aforementioned fondness. I like Korik, Hyrim, and Shetra, and have always grieved over the exigency which required me to reduce their role in the story so drastically. But, in addition, I've often felt that the moral dilemma of the Bloodguard is somewhat obscure in the published version of my books: too much of their background was sacrificed when I cut GILDEN-FIRE. In fact, too much development of the people who would eventually have to face the destruction of the Unhomed was sacrificed. (How, for instance, can Lord Hyrim's achievements be fully understood when so little is known about him?) By publishing GILDEN-FIRE, I'm trying to fill a subtle but real gap in THE ILLEARTH WAR.

Finally, I should say that I think the logic which originally required me to cut out this material no longer applies. Since it cannot stand on its own as an independent story, GILDEN-FIRE will surely not be read by anyone unfamiliar with 'The Chronicles of Thomas Covenant the Unbeliever'. And those readers know that the question of whether or not the Land is ultimately 'real' (whether or not a character like Korik is sufficiently 'actual' to serve as a narrative view-point) no longer matters. In reality as in dreams, what matters is the answer we find in our hearts to the test of Despite. By publishing GILDEN-FIRE, I hope to give more substance to the answers Korik, Hyrim, and Shetra found.

GILDEN-FIRE

GILDEN-FIRE

S SUNRISE ECHOED the fire of farewell
which High Lord Elena had laun-
ched into the heavens from the
watchtower of Revelstone, Korik
Bloodguard and his mission to Seareach
wheeled their Ranyhyn, tightened their resolve
about them, and went running into the east.

With the new sun in his eyes, Korik could
not see clearly. Yet he moved comfortably to the
rhythm of Brabha's strides, faced the prospect
ahead without a qualm. He had been riding
Brabha for nearly fifty years now; but his experience of Ranyhyn was far longer than that:
the great horses of Ra by the score had borne
him in turn, one after another as their individual lives ended and their fidelity passed from
generation to generation. He knew that the
Ranyhyn would not miss their footing. The

terrain near Revelstone was much-travelled
and reliable; yet even in the cluttered rigour of
the Northron Climbs, or in the subtle decep-
tions of Sarangrave Flat, the Ranyhyn would
remain sure-footed. Their instincts were found-
ed on something more constant than the super-
ficial details of hills and plains. They bore
Korik's mission down through the foothills of
Revelstone as confidently as if the great horses
were part of the ground itself – a part made
mobile and distinct by their quicker life-pulse,
but still sharing the same bone, the same ances-
try, so that no orphaning misstep or betrayal
could occur between hoof and earth.

And around Korik rode his companions,
those who shared his mission to the Giants
of Seareach: fourteen more Bloodguard and two
Lords, Hyrim son of Hoole, and Shetra Verement-mate. The memory of their parting from
the people of Revelstone – Shetra's grief over
her separation from her un-Ranyhyn-chosen
and self-doubting husband, Hyrim's argute
attempts to probe the difference between what
the Bloodguard remembered and what they

knew, Thomas Covenant's refusal to share this mission – was vivid to Korik. But more vivid still was the urgent need which gave cause to this journey. Summon or succour. A need so compulsory that it had been given into his hands, to the Bloodguard themselves, rather than to the Lords, so that if Hyrim or Shetra fell their defenders would go on.

For there had been a special timbre of exigency in Terrel's silent voice earlier that night as he had sent out his call to First Mark Morin.

– Summon the High Lord, Terrel had said, following a grim-eyed and haggard Lord Mhoram toward the Close. There is a peril upon the Giants of Seareach. He has seen it.

Lord Mhoram had seen it. Seer and oracle to the Council, he had described the death of the Unhomed stalking them across all the leagues between Revelstone and *Coercri* – a death no more distant than a score of days. When the High Lord and all the Council had gathered with him in the Close, he had told them what he had seen. His vision had left them grey with many kinds of dread.

In this Korik knew the Lords well. Without sleep or let, he had served the Council in all its manifestions for two millenia: he knew that the pain in Hyrim and Callindrill and Mhoram, the bitten hardness of Shetra and Verement, the wide alarm of the Lords Amatin, Loerya, and Trevor arose from concern for the life-loving Unhomed – a concern as deep as the ancient friendship and fealty between the Giants and the Land. But Korik also understood the other dreads. Corruption was mustering war against the Council; and that jeopardy had become so imminent that only scant days ago the High Lord had felt compelled to summon the Unbeliever from his unwilling world. In such a need, all the eyes of the Land naturally turned toward Seareach for assistance. And for three years there had been silence between the Giants and Revelstone.

A year of silence was not unusual. Therefore the first year had not been questioned. But the second gave birth to anxiety, and so messengers were dispatched to Seareach. None of them

returned. In the third year, one Eoman was sent
– and not seen again. Unwilling to hazard more
of the Warward, the High Lord had then commanded the Lords Callindrill and Amatin to
carry word of the Land's need eastward. But
they had been turned back by Sarangrave Flat;
and still the silence endured. Thus the Council
had already known fear for the Giants as well as
for themselves. Lord Mhoram's vision gave
that fear substance.

The High Lord did not hesitate to conceive
aid for the Giants. Summon or succour. But
Corruption's hordes were believed to be march-
ing for the Land's ruin; and few warriors and
little power could be spared from the defence.
So the mission was given to the Bloodguard.
Given by First Mark Morin to Korik by reason
of his rank and years. And by the High Lord to
the Lords Hyrim and Shetra: Hyrim son of
Hoole, a corpulent, humorous, and untried
man with an avowed passion for all fleshly
comforts and a silent love of Giants; and Shetra
Verement-mate, whose pain at her husband's
self-doubt made her as bitter as the hawk she

resembled. It was a small force to hurl into the unknown path of Corruption's malice. No Bloodguard required reminder that there were only two roads to bear the Despiser westward; one to the south of Andelain, then northward against Revelstone; the other to the north of Mount Thunder, then westward through Grimmerdhore Forest. And Korik's way toward Seareach also lay through Grimmerdhore.

However, the road of Corruption's choice was uncertain; and the Bloodguard did not pang themselves with uncertainties. Korik and his people were not required by their Vow to know the unknown: they were required only to succeed or die. It was not in that fashion that they had been taught doubt. The test of their service was one of judgment rather than knowledge.

When Korik left the Close, he went without hesitation about the task of selecting his comrades.

He had no qualm about his choices: the Bloodguard shared a community of prowess and responsibility; and any individual member of the community could be elected or replaced without causing any falter in the service of the Vow. Yet he exercised care in his decisions. Cerrin and Sill he included as a matter of course: they had borne the direct care of Shetra and Hyrim since those Lords had first joined the Council. Then he added Runnik and Pren because they were among the senior members of the two ancient *Haruchai* clans, the *Ho-aru* and *Nimishi*, that in the mountain fastnesses of their home had warred together for generations until the Bond which had united them. Similarly, he included five younger Bloodguard from each clan, so that both would have a fair hand in the mission. Among these was Tull, the youngest of the Bloodguard.

Some time ago, when Lord Mhoram had made his scouting sojourn to the Spoiled Plains and Hotash Slay, and had been forced to flee, the Bloodguard with him had fallen. In keeping with the ritual of the Vow, the fallen had been Ranyhyn-borne to Guards Gap and the Westron Mountains for burial in native grave-grounds, and the *Haruchai* had sent new men to replace them. Tull was among them. He was centuries younger than Korik; and though the Vow bound him and straitened him and sustained him and kept him from sleep, so that he was a Bloodguard like any other, still he did not know the Giants as his older comrades did. For this reason, Korik chose him. It would gratify Tull to see that the unflawed fealty of the Bloodguard was not unmatched: the Giants of Seareach could also be trusted beyond any possibility of Corruption.

As he walked soundlessly through the halls of Revelstone, sending out his mental summons, Korik considered the advantages in taking either Morril or Koral with him. They were the Bloodguard who watched over the Lords Callindrill and Amatin: Morril and Koral had accompanied those Lords when they had attempted to reach the Giants and were driven back by some lurking power in the Sarangrave. Both these Bloodguard had previous experience with the dangers which faced the mission. But Korik had heard all that Morril and Koral could tell concerning the danger. And they had the right to remain with the Lords whom they had personally warded.

The choosing completed, Korik went to the place where his comrades would meet him – the one place in Revelstone reserved for the Bloodguard. It was a dim uncompromising hall, with unrubbed walls and a rough raw floor on which no one but a Bloodguard would walk barefoot. The whole space was unfurnished and unadorned, but it served them as it was. They needed only an open space with a punishing floor and freedom from observation.

Korik did not have to wait long for his chosen comrades. They came promptly, though without any appearance of hurry, for the word of Mhoram's vision had gone out ahead of Korik's summons: they had heard it in the mental talk of the *Haruchai*, in the orders of the Lords, in the altered and quickened beat of Revelstone's rhythms. But when Cerrin and Sill, Runnik and Pren, Tull and the others gathered around him, Korik still took the time to speak to them. The mission which First Mark

Morin had given him was special, perhaps higher than any other burden the Bloodguard would bear in this war. Their responsibility had always been to the Lords: they had Vowed to preserve the Lords while the Council went about its work. Rarely had any Bloodguard been given a command which was not part of his direct service. But the mission to the Giants had been entrusted to the *Haruchai*. Summon or succour. To meet this uncommon charge, Korik gathered his company about him for old rites.

– Faith, he greeted them.

– Fist and faith, they replied together.

– Hail, chosen brothers, Korik returned. The mission to the Giants of Seareach is in our hands. These are Bloodguard times. War marches. The end of the Giants' exile is near, as foretold by Damelon Giantfriend. Dour fist and unbroken faith prevail.

The Bloodguard answered in the words of the ancient *Haruchai* Vow:

– *Ha-man rual tayba-sah carab ho-eeal neeta par-raoul.* We are the Bloodguard, the keepers of the Vow – the keepers and the kept, sanctified beyond decline and the last evil of death. *Tan-Haruchai*. We accept.

– *Tan-Haruchail*, Korik said. Bowing to his comrades, he repeated the old war-cry: Fist and faith!

They bowed in turn, stepped back so that there was a clear space around him. Then they began the trial of leadership, as prescribed by the rites he had invoked. One by one, they came forward to fight with him, to measure their strength against his.

Although he had been given the mission by the First Mark, Korik wanted to affirm his leadership among his company, so that in any future extremity no question of his right to command could arise. Therefore he fought for his leadership as he had once fought to be among the commanders of the army which had invaded the Land in the early years of High Lord Kevin son of Loric.

This trial came instinctively to the proud *Haruchai*, for they had been born to fighting in the same way that their forefathers had been born to it, and their forefathers before them, as the old tellers described. For them, it was not enough that they made their home in one of the most demanding places of the Earth. It was not enough that the fastnesses which they in- habited, the caves and crags, the ice-grottoes and crevasses and eyries, were snow-locked three seasons a year and in places perpetually clamped in blue glaciers – that simple survival from day to day, the preservation of the home- fires, and the tending of the goats and the bare gardening they did when in summer some of the valleys were free of snow and ice, took all the strength and fortitude which any people could ask of themselves – that blizzards and mountain winds and avalanches provided them with so much disaster that even the hardiest and most cunning of them could not look to have a long life. No, in addition the *Haruchai* were always at war.

Before the Bond, they had fought each other, battling *Ho-aru* against *Nimishi*, genera- tion after generation, across cliffs and cols and scree and ravines, wherever they met. They were a hot people, strong-loined and prolific:

Then they began the trial of leadership,
as prescribed by the rites he had invoked.

but without food and shelter and warmth, children died at birth – and often the women died as well. Caught thus constantly between the need to replenish the people and the mortality of love, the clans strove to wrest every possible scrap of food or flicker of heat or shadow of shelter from each other, so that their wives and children might not die.

Yet in time a kind of understanding came to the *Ho-aru* and *Nimishi*. They saw that they fought a feud they could not win. First, the clans were too evenly matched for one side to retain for long any brief ascendance. And second, even victory offered no solution to the need, for a victorious family would quickly grow in size until it was as large as two; and then the lack of food and warmth and shelter would kill as before. So the leaders of the clans met and formed the Bond. Emnity was set aside, and hands were joined. From that time onward, *Ho-aru* and *Nimishi* warred together against their common need.

That need sent them eastward, out of the Westron Mountains, intending to conquer by might of fist the forms of sustenance their home did not provide, so that their wives and children would live. Korik had fought his way through a trial of leadership lasting an entire winter to gain a place – with Tuvor, Bannor, Morin, and Terrel – among the commanders of the army which had marched, a thousand strong, through Guards Gap and along the glacial purity of the Llurallin River, to wage war against the Land.

They passed without resistance across the region which was later to be named Kurash Plenethor, Stricken Stone, and Trothgard. Seeking battle, they were received by the inhabitants with quiet and fearless tolerance, were given without struggle all they demanded. These peaceful people had no use for war. Eventually, they even guided the *Haruchai* to Revelstone, where the Council of High Lord Kevin was still in its youth.

There began the stuff of which the Bloodguard Vow, and the fealty between the Giants and the *Haruchai*, were made.

Revelstone itself met the eyes of the in-

[29]

vaders with a wonder such as they had never known. They understood mountains, cliffs, indomitable stone, and never in their warmest dreams had they conceived that gutrock could be so made welcoming, habitable, and extravagant. The great Giant-wrought Keep astonished them, inspired them with a fierce joy unmatched by anything except the sight of austere peaks majestically facing heavenward and the enfolding love of wives. And the more they looked, the more ecstatic Revelstone appeared. Half intuitively, they sensed the pattern, the commingling flow and rest of the balconies and coigns and windows and parapets, which the Giants had woven into the rock of the high walls – perceived it dimly, and were enthralled. Here, amid warmth and lushness and fertility and food and sunlight, was a single rock home capacious enough to enclose the entire *Haruchai* people and hold them free of want forever. The suggestiveness of such luxurience made the very crenellations of the battlements seem luminous, strangely lit by high mysteries and unquenchable possibilities.

In the rush of their unfamiliar passion, they swore an oath that they would conquer this Keep and make it their own. Without hesitation, one thousand unarmed *Haruchai* laid siege to Revelstone.

Their war-making did not go far. Almost at once, the great stone gates under the watchtower swung wide, and High Lord Kevin rode out to meet his besiegers. He was mounted on a grand Ranyhyn and accompanied by half his Council, one Eoman of the Warward, and a coterie of grinning Giants. Solemnly, Kevin listened while First Mark Tuvor delivered his terms of war; and some power of the Staff of Law enabled the High Lord to understand the *Haruchai* tongue. Then he declared so all the *Haruchai* might grasp his meaning that under no circumstances would he fight the invaders. He declined to make war. Instead, he invited the five commanders into Revelstone to the hospitality of the Lords. And though they expected treachery, they accepted, because they were proud.

But there was no treachery. The great

gates stood open for three days while the
Haruchai commanders tasted the grandeur of
Revelstone. They experienced the laughing ge-
nial power of the Giants who had made the
Keep, received the confident offer of Kevin's
Council to supply the *Haruchai* freely whatever
they needed for as long as their need lasted.
When the commanders returned to their army,
they sat astride prancing Ranyhyn, which had
come from the Plains of Ra at Kevin's call and
had chosen to bear the *Haruchai*. Korik and his
peers were of one mind. Something new was
upon them, something beyond instinctive
kinship with the Ranyhyn, beyond friendship
and awe for the Giants, beyond even the fine
entrancement of Revelstone itself. The *Haruchai*
were fighters, accustomed to wrest what they
required: they could not accept gifts without
making meet return.

Therefore that night the army from the
Westron Mountains gathered under the south
wall of Revelstone. All the *Haruchai* joined their
minds together and out of their common
strength forged the metal of the Vow – un-

alloyed and unanswerable, accessible to no appeal or flaw, unambergrised by the promise of any uncorrupt end: a Vow like the infernal oath upon the river of death which binds even the gods. This they wrought out of the extremity and innocence of their hearts, to match the handiwork of the Giants and the mastery of the Lords. As they spoke the hot words – *Ha-man rual tayba-sah carab ho-eeal* – the ground seemed to grow hot and cognizant under their feet, as if the Earthpower were drawing near the surface to hear them. And when they brought their Vow around full circle, sealing it so that there was no escape, the rocks on which they stood thundered, and fire ran through them, sealing their bones to the promise they had made.

Thus it was done. Before dawn, the remainder of the army marched away toward Guards Gap and home. The five hundred *Haruchai* of the Vow went to Revelstone to become the Bloodguard, defenders of the Lords: the last preserving wall between Revelstone and any blot or stain.

Yet that was not all. Though Korik now on

the eve of the mission to Seareach invoked the old trial of leadership to test his place in the company he had chosen – though the Vow he served was as always impeccable and binding – yet the history of the Bloodguard contained at least two other matters which each of them kept in account. The first of these came at once, the morning after the Vow was taken. When the *Haruchai* entered Revelstone and announced their purpose to the Council, High Lord Kevin was dismayed. Like the Lord Mhoram in the later age, Kevin was at times gifted or blighted with presciences; and he treated the Vow as if it proferred disaster. He insisted strangely that the *Haruchai* had maimed themselves: he strove to refuse the service, so much was he taken aback – and so little did he understand the fierce hearts of these people. But the Giants taught him to understand, and to accept.

The second matter arose from the last war, before Kevin chose to enact the Ritual of Desecration. When the High Lord knew in secret what he purposed, he set about saving as much of the Land as he could. He forewarned the Giants and Ranyhyn, so that they might flee the coming havoc. And he ordered the Bloodguard away, into the safety of the mountains.

This was the question which now plagued the Bloodguard, taught them doubt, this question of judgment. They had obeyed the High Lord, and so survived the Desecration; but the Lords to whom they had sworn their service were lost. The Bloodguard had obeyed because they had never considered that Kevin might wish to thwart their Vow. Even now the fact felt inconceivable, threatening. They had trusted him, assumed that his orders were consonant with their intent. Now they knew otherwise. Kevin had prevented them from dying with him – or from opposing his dark purpose. He had betrayed them.

Now the Bloodguard knew how to doubt. And now their Vow had revealed an additional demand: to fulfill it, they must preserve the Lords from self-destruction.

Therefore Korik invoked the rites of leadership. He remembered his whole history –

the Vow gave no relief from memory – and because of it he acted as he did. He raised hands which knew how to kill against his comrades.

He did not hold back his strength, or cover his blows, or in any other way fight less fiercely than he would have fought a foe of the Lords. There was no need for restraint: there were no frail or unskilled fighters among the Blood-guard; their devotion to the Vow kept their alertness keen and their thews strong. And the first tests were not long. Runnik and Pren were veterans of the Bloodguard, had measured their strength against his often enough to know him exactly. After a few swift passes, they acknow-ledged that he was the same warrior who had bested them before. And in deference to their example, the younger *Ho-aru* and *Nimishi* also contented themselves with fleet, flurrying ripostes to demonstrate Korik's worthiness – and their own. Cerrin and Sill took longer, more because they respected the Lords they warded than because they desired to take away Korik's command. But he had been one of the original *Haruchai* commanders for good reason. Fighting with a speed which masked the precision of his movements, he showed Cerrin and Sill in turn that he remained one of the elite.

When they were satisfied, Korik encountered Tull.

He was gratified by the strength of Tull's metal. In many ways, Tull was still an untried Bloodguard; and because of this, Korik attacked him relentlessly. But Tull quickly showed that over the generations the *Haruchai* had not been content with old skills: they had developed new counters and blows, new feints and angles of attack. In moments, Korik was pushed to his limits, and Tull seemed to have the upper hand. But Korik had experienced conflict against many different and versatile opponents. He learned swiftly. When an unusual feint caught him, knocked him back, he spun and twisted, avoided the fall which would have signalled his defeat. Then he met Tull with the same feint. The blow stretched Tull on the rough floor, and the trial was over.

Tull bounded to his feet, stood with the other Bloodguard facing Korik.

– Fist and faith, they said. We are the Bloodguard. *Tan-Haruchai.*

– *Tan-Haruchail*, Korik acknowledged. He bowed slightly to his comrades, and they followed him from the chamber. Among them, he was the only one whose pulse or breathing had quickened; but outwardly he revealed nothing of the trial of leadership.

When his company regained the main halls of Revelstone, they separated to gather supplies. For themselves they would carry nothing but raiment and long coils of *clingor*, the adhesive leather rope which had been introduced to the Land by the Giants. They bore no weapons. And, in part because of their Vow, they needed little food: as long as the hardy *aliantha* grew and ripened throughout the Land in all seasons, the Bloodguard required no other sustenance. But the Lords would need more equipage: food and drink, *lillianrill* rods for torches, some *graveling*, bedding, cookware, a few knives and other utensils. Such things the Bloodguard would carry on their backs, so that Shetra and Hyrim would not be wearied by

packs. Other resources Korik left to the Lords.
He took care of the needs within his power.

Those which were not did not trouble him.
He had no answer for Lord Shetra's dour dismay – though he had paid for centuries the cost
of the yearning between a man and a woman –
and so he stood aloof from it. He had no hand in
the unvoiced fear which caused Lord Hyrim to
ask Thomas Covenant's company in defiance of
the High Lord's wishes: therefore he made no
effort to sway or deny the Unbeliever. And he
fended away all questions which ranged beyond
the ambit of his certainty. Fist and faith. Succeed or die. Aided by the native flatness of his
features, he bore himself as if he possessed no
emotions which might be touched.

Yet he grieved for Shetra and respected
Hyrim. He judged the Unbeliever coldly. And
the arrival of the Ranyhyn, seventeen of the
great horses of Ra with their starred foreheads
and their strange responsive fidelity, thunder-
ing forward in the first hint of day in answer to
his call – that pride and beauty was a hymn in
his heart. He was *Haruchai* and Bloodguard. His

people had shown in their Vow how extremely they could be touched.

Thus now there was a special revelling in him as Brabha bore him down out of the foot-hills of Lord's Keep into the lower plains, the easy farmlands which spread for leagues on all the eastern slopes. There he and his compan-ions began to encounter brief villages – small clustered Stonedowns and an occasional Woodhelven in the old spread banyan trees which dotted this part of the plains, homes for the farmers and artisans who, despite their vital share in the life of Revelstone, preferred not to live in that massed habitation. In the dim dawn light, the riders slowed their pace to a more cautious trot, so that they ran no risk of tram-pling a groggy farmer or child. But when the sun came up fully, the Ranyhyn greeted it with glad nickering, as if they were welcoming an old dear friend, and stretched their strides again.

In the fresh day, the countryside shone as if it were oblivious to the looming threat of blood. Ripe wheat rippled like sheets of gold in some of the fields; and in others cut hay was stacked into high fragrant mowes. Over them, the air blew its autumn nip: the breeze carried the smells of the crops like a counterpoint to the morning enthusiasm of the birds. The farmland seemed to defy the spectre which hunted it. Korik knew better: he had seen land as fair as this helpless to withstand fire and trampling and the thick unhealthy drench of blood. But he did not forget, could never forget, the heart-wrench of beauty which had in part brought the *Haruchai* to their Vow. It baffled expression, surpassed any language but its own. He understood the overflowing mood which caused Lord Hyrim to throw back his head and sing as if he were crowing:

'Hail! Weal!
Land and Life!
Pulse of power in tree and stone!
Earth-heart-blood
vital, vivid surge
in pith and rock!
Sun-warmth
balm-bliss bless

all air and sea and lung and life!
Land's soul's beauty!
Skyweir
Earthroot
weal!
Hail!'

The song had a strange power to catch its
hearers, as if it actively desired them to join it;
and Lord Hyrim relished it. But Shetra did not
smile or sing or even look toward Hyrim. She
rode on grimly, as if the war were already upon
her. This also Korik understood. He sat between them comprehending and mute.

Thus they rode through the morning until
the swift roaming gait of the Ranyhyn had
placed most of the fields and villages behind
them and the terrain began to give hints of its
coming roughness. Lord Hyrim alternately
sang and talked as if all the countryside were his
enchanted audience; but Lord Shetra and the
Bloodguard moved in their private silences.

Then towards noon they stopped beside a
stream to give the Lords rest and the Ranyhyn

chance to graze. Hyrim's awkward dismount confirmed an impression which had been growing on Korik: although the Lord had been freely chosen by the Ranyhyn, he was an unusually poor rider. Even an inexperienced person could sit safely on a Ranyhyn if he left himself in the horse's care. And Lord Hyrim was not inexperienced. Yet he rode with erratic jerks, as if repeatedly he lost his balance and nearly fell. His dismount was only half a matter of choice. Korik thought of the hard riding ahead and winced inwardly.

– He has always ridden thus, Sill answered. His balance is faulty. Almost the tests of the Sword in the Loresraat defeated him, prevented him from Lordship.

– Yet the Ranyhyn selected him, Korik mused.

– Their judgement is sure.

– Yes, Korik replied after a moment. And his Ranyhyn knows the danger.

Nevertheless he felt anxiety. He wondered if the High Lord had known of Hyrim's deficiency as a rider. If she had, why had she chosen him? However, such questions were not within Korik's responsibility, and he recited his Vow to silence them. The mission would give him the measure of Lord Hyrim's fitness.

Hyrim himself was obviously aware of the problem. He limped ruefully away from the Ranyhyn and dropped flat on his stomach to drink from the stream. After a long draught, he pushed himself onto his back, spat a last mouthful of water over the grass, and groaned, 'By the Seven! Is it only noon? Half of one day? Friend Korik, how long will we require to gain Seareach?'

Korik shrugged. 'Perhaps less than a score of days – if we are not delayed.'

'A score –? *Melenkurion!* Then let us pray that we are not delayed. A score of days' – he sat up with a huge show of difficulty – 'will leave me eighteen in my grave.'

'Then,' said Shetra sourly, 'we will be the first folk in life to hear a dead man complain for eighteen days.'

At this, Lord Hyrim fell back to the grass, laughing gleefully.

Thus they rode through the morning until
the terrain began to give hints of its coming roughness.

When his mirth had subsided, he rolled his
eyes at Shetra and attempted to stand up
smoothly, as if he were not sore and tired. But
he could not do it: a spasm of strain broke across
his face, and he started to laugh again, as if his
own pretensions were the most innocent enter-
tainment imaginable. Still chuckling, he limped
away to a nearby *aliantha* and fed himself on the
viridian berries of the gnarled bush, savouring
their crisp tangy flavour and the rush of nour-
ishment they gave him. Scrupulously, he observed the custom of the Land by scattering the
seeds around him, so that new bushes might
grow. Then with a flourish he indicated his readiness to ride on. In moments, the company
was mounted again and cantering eastward.

As they travelled, they moved into sterner
countryside, land which was only hospitable to
people who knew how to husband it. And they
met with fewer villages. By evening, they were
beyond the range of Revelstone's immediate
influence; and before the gloaming had thickened into darkness they had passed the last
human habitation between that region and

Grimmerdhore Forest. Yet they did not stop, though Lord Hyrim suggested the possibility with a genuine yearning in his voice. Korik kept the company riding in spite of Hyrim's groans. So they continued into the night, trusting the Ranyhyn to find their way. Moonrise was near when Lord Shetra said in a low, measured tone, 'Now we must rest. We must have strength for the morrow and Grimmerdhore.' Korik agreed: he did not miss the point of her glance toward Hyrim.

When his mount finally came to a halt, Lord Hyrim fell off as if he were already unconscious, moaning in his sleep.

– Is his pain severe? Korik asked Sill.

– No, Sill responded. He is unaccustomed. He will recover. But he will have difficulty in Grimmerdhore.

Korik nodded. He said farewell to Brabha for the night and began unwrapping the bundle on his back. The other Bloodguard followed his example: soon all the Ranyhyn had galloped away to feed and rest, and to keep a distant watch over the camp. When the *lillianrill* rods were unpacked, Lord Shetra used one to start a small campfire. With some of the supplies Korik had brought, she cooked a sparse meal. While she ate, she watched Lord Hyrim as if she expected the smell of the food to rouse him. But he remained face down on the grass, whimpering softly from time to time. Finally, she went to him and nudged him with her foot.

He shoved himself up sharply, clutched his staff as if he had been snatched out of sleep to face an attack. For a dazed instant, his lips trembled, and his eyes rolled widely. But when he gained his feet, he awoke enough to see where he was. The fear faded from his face, leaving it grey and weak. Heavily, he shambled to the fire, sat down, and ate what Shetra had left for him.

However, the food seemed to meet his needs. Soon he recovered enough cheerfulness to groan, 'Sister Shetra, you are not a good cook.'

When she made no reply, he stretched himself on his back by the fire, sighing plaintively, 'Ah, agony!' For a time, he stared at the way the flames danced without consuming along the special wood of the *lillianrill*. Then he turned his face to the sky and said gruffly, 'Friends, I had bethought me of fit revenge against those who gave to me this unendurable ride. Since noon, I have been full of dire promises – in place of food, I think. But now I am contrite. The fault is mine alone. I have been a fat thistle-brained fool from the moment the thought of the Loresraat and Lordship entered my head. Ah, what business had I to dream of Lords and Giants, of lore and bold undertakings? Better had I been punished severely and sent to tend sheep for the rest of my days, rather than permitted to follow mad fancies. But Hoole Gren-mate my father was a kind man, slow to chastise. Alas, his memory is poorly honoured in my thick self. Were he to see me now, thus reduced to raw quivering flesh and strengthless bones by one single day astride the honour of a Ranyhyn, he would have shed great fat tears as a reproach to my overfed resourcelessness.'

'Then let us rejoice in his absence,' said

Shetra distantly. 'I do not like tears.'

Hyrim took this up as if it were an argument. 'That is well for you. You are brave of blood and limb – in every way enviably courageous. But I – do you hear the talk of the refectories in Revelstone? It is said there that my staff is warped – that when this staff was made for me by High Lord Osondrea, it felt the touch of my hand and bent itself in chagrin. By the Seven! I would be offended if only the talk were untrue. I weep at every opportunity.'

He looked over at Shetra to see if he had produced any effect. But she appeared to be listening to some other voice, and she spoke as if to herself. 'Am I?'

'Are you?' Hyrim inquired gently. But when she did not reply, he returned to his badinage. 'Are you courageous? – is that your question? Sister Shetra, I assure you! I have proof positive. Who but a woman with bravery in her very marrow would consent to share such a mission with me?'

At this, Lord Shetra turned her bird-of-prey eyes toward Hyrim. 'You mock me.'

'Ah, no!' he protested at once. 'Do not think it. You must learn to hear me in my own spirit. I seek only to warm the air between us.'

'Better that you do not speak,' she snapped. 'I do not hear your desires. The wind of your words blows cold.'

Instead of replying, Lord Hyrim gazed at her with the look of intent repose which came over the Lords when they melded their thoughts. She shook her head, refused him, climbed to her feet. But the next moment, she answered him barrenly, as if she were too full of dust to resist his question. 'I have left behind a husband who believes I cannot love him. He believes he is inferior to me.'

She cut off any response Hyrim might have made by stepping quickly to the fire. 'We must not keep the wood alight more than necessary. Without a Hirebrand to tend them, the rods will decay slowly – and we will have greater need of them.' As if she were in a hurry for darkness, she pulled the wood out of the fire and hummed a *lillianrill* command to extinguish it. Then she wrapped herself in a blanket and lay

down on the grass a short distance from Lord
Hyrim.

After a while, Korik asked Cerrin:

– Will her concern for Lord Verement
weaken her?

– No, Cerrin replied flatly. She will fight
for both.

Korik understood this assertion and
accepted it. But he did not like it. It carried
echoes of other losses and griefs – deprivations
and hollow places which the *Haruchai* had not
taken into account during their sole night of
extravagance. Dourly, he posted his comrades
in a wide circle around the camp. Then he stood
with his arms folded on his chest, gazed warily
out over the grasslands and the star-path of the
moon, recited his Vow through the long watch.
He could not forget any details of the last night
he had spent with his wife, whose bones were
already ancient in the frozen fastness of her
grave. The Vow sustained him, but it was not
warm.

Still, it gave a rhythm to the sleepless
night, and the time passed as a myriad other

darknesses had passed – in ceaseless vigilance.
When the moon completed its worn traversal of
the sky and fell into the west like a weary
exhalation, Korik decided that soon he would
awaken the Lords. However, a short time later
Lord Hyrim struggled out of his blankets of his
own accord. Even in the bare starlight, Korik
saw that Hyrim was stiff and aching from the
past day's ride. But the Lord suppressed the
groans which twisted his face, and began to
prepare breakfast.

The aroma he created revealed his talent
for the work. Korik smelled strength and re-
freshment and delicacy in the steam of the broth
Hyrim made – a savour Korik had not scented
since the curious healing meal which High Lord
Prothall had cooked after the battle of Soaring
Woodhelven, when all the warriors and ur-
Lord Covenant were sickened by the reek of
blood and burned flesh. The food's subtle
potency awakened Lord Shetra. She came close
to the fire looking dull and pale, as if she had not
slept well for many nights; but as she ate,
Hyrim's work spread its beneficence through

her, and she brightened. When she was done, she nodded to him, approving the food as if she were aplogizing. He answered with a broad grin and an apothegm which he claimed he had learned from the Giants:

'Food is concentrated beauty – the sustaining power of the Land made savourable and ready for strength. A life without food is like a life without tales – deprived of splendour.'

When he mounted to ride again, he managed to limit himself to one tight gasp of pain.

The Ranyhyn ran as if they were hurrying to rejoin the sun; and at daybreak the riders found that they were crossing short irregular hills covered with stiff grey grass. There was no sign of human life. The ground was arable, if not inviting; but no people had ever lived here. It was too close to Grimmerdhore. Though dark, Grimmerdhore was among the least potent, the most slumberous, of the Forests, the surviving remnants of the One Forest which had formerly covered the whole Upper Land – and though since before the time of Lord Kevin there had been no Forestal in Grimmerdhore to

sing the ancient trees to wakefulness and move-
ment and vengeance – still people kept away
from the severe woods. Many things lived in
Grimmerdhore, and few of them were friendly.
It was said – though Korik did not know the
truth of it – that the *kresh*, the yellow wolves, had
been born in Grimmerdhore.

Yet the Bloodguard did not waver in his
determination to pass directly through the
Forest. It would lengthen the journey by days to
go around, either north or south. Still, he exercised added caution. As the company cantered
into the new day, Korik sent one of his comrades wide of the company on each side, to
increase the range of their wariness.

By midmorning, his caution was re-
warded. Korik received a call from one of the
ranging Bloodguard, who was out of sight behind a hill. He stopped the company and
waited. When the caller came over the hill, he
was accompanied by a woman mounted on a
Revelstone mustang.

She was a brisk young Warhaft, and her
Eoman was riding patrol along the western

borders of Grimmerdhore. She asked for news
of Revelstone, and when she heard of Lord
Mhoram's vision, she requested permission to
accompany the mission. But Lord Shetra
ordered the Warhaft to remain at her scouting
duty, then inquired about the condition of
Grimmerdhore.

'Wolves,' the Warhaft reported. 'Not the
yellow *kresh*. Grey and black wolves – nothing
else. And little of them. Small packs raid out-
ward, find nothing and return. We have
avoided them so that they would not be wary of
our scouting.'

'No sign of the Grey Slayer?' Shetra pur-
sued. 'No scent of evil?'

'The Forest conceals much. But we have
seen nothing – heard nothing.'

The Warhaft and Shetra exchanged a few
more details, and the Lord refused an offer of
help for the crossing of Grimmerdhore. Then
the mission started eastward again. As they left
the Warhaft behind, Hyrim waved back at her
and said as if he were lonely, 'It may be that we
will see no other people until we gain Seareach.

I would have been glad for the company of her Eoman.'

'They would slow us,' Shetra returned without looking at him.

Korik sent two Bloodguard wide again. In this formation, he was confident of the company's readiness except on one point: Lord Hyrim's horsemanship. Since the previous day, Hyrim's scant control over his riding had deteriorated – the combined effect of rougher terrain and extreme soreness. Now at every jolt he clutched like a drowning man at the mane of the Ranyhyn; and between grasps he used his staff like a pole to steady himself.

– If he falls, I will catch him, Sill promised.

But Korik was not reassured.

– At full gallop in Grimmerdhore, he will be at hazard.

Sill stiffened, but could not deny Korik's point. He proposed constructing a harness for the Lord, then discarded the idea. The Bloodguard had no wish to affront the Ranyhyn that had chosen Hyrim: they preferred to carry the additional risk themselves. Korik drew calmness from his Vow and observed to his comrades that the question of Hyrim's riding would soon be answered.

Just before noon, the company swept over a ridge and came within sight of the Forest. The hills had hidden it until it was almost upon them. It loomed around them on the east and south as if they had surprised it in the act of trying to encircle them. But now that they had seen it, Grimmerdhore Forest stood up out of the grasslands like a fortress: its black trunks grew thickly together as if to form a wall; its gnarled limbs bristled like weapons; its shrouding dark green seemed to shelter lurking defenders. And over all the ground before and between the trees were brambles with barbed thorns as strong as iron. They interwove with each other tightly, to resist any penetration, and at their lowest they were taller than Korik.

The Ranyhyn stopped, unbidden: they were sensitive to the denying will of the Forest, though the trees had never held any enmity for them. The riders dismounted. Lord Hyrim stared at Grimmerdhore as if its mood confounded him; and Lord Shetra dropped to the grass, felt it with her hands, staring all the while at the trees – trying to read the Forest through the sensations in the ground. When Hyrim said, 'Never have I seen Grimmerdhore so angry,' she nodded slowly and replied, 'Something has been done to it – something it does not like.'

Korik was forced to agree. In the past, the ancient ire of the Forest, the hatred for people who cut and burned, had always been drowsier than this, more deeply submerged in the failing consciousness of the trees. Still, what he could see of Grimmerdhore did not look sentient enough to be active.

– Then the peril lies in what has been done to the Forest, said Tull, completing Korik's thought.

– Unless a Forestal has found his way here, Runnik suggested.

– No, Korik judged. Even a Forestal would require much time to awaken Grimmerdhore. There is another danger within.

Gradually, the Lords began to resist the

mood of the Forest. Hyrim started to prepare a meal – a large one, since he would not have the use of a cooking fire again until the company was past Grimmerdhore – and Shetra walked to the brambles to touch them with her fingertips and listen to the murmurings of the wind. When she returned, she had reached Korik's conclusion: there was not enough wakefulness in the timbre of the wood to account for Grimmerdhore's mood. Something else caused it.

'Not the wolves,' said Hyrim, sampling his fare. 'They have always been at home in the Forest. And they care for nothing but themselves – unless another power is there to master them. Another mystery I hope I will not be asked to unravel. Riding is challenge enough for me.' Shetra nodded absently, ate the food Hyrim gave her without paying it much attention.

In spite of their concern, the Lords did not delay. They ate promptly, then left the Bloodguard to pack their supplies and went together on foot to the edge of the brambles. There they raised their arms, held their staffs high, and gave the ritual appeal for sufferance to the woods:

'Hail, Grimmerdhore! Forest of the One Forest! Freehome and root, and preserver of the life-sap of wood! Enemy of our enemies! Grimmerdhore, hail! We are the Lords – foes to your enemies, and learners of the *lillianrill* lore. We must pass through!

'Harken, Grimmerdhore! We hate the axe and flame which hurt you! Your enemies are our enemies. Never have we brought edge of axe of flame of fire to touch you – nor ever shall. Grimmerdhore, harken! Let us pass!'

They shouted the appeal loudly; but their cry was cut off, absorbed into silence, by the wall of the trees. Still they waited with their arms raised for a long moment, as if they expected an answer. But the dark anger of the Forest did not waver. When they returned to the company, Lord Shetra said squarely to Korik, 'Grimmerdhore Forest has never harmed the Lords of its own will. What is your choice, Bloodguard? Shall we attempt passage?'

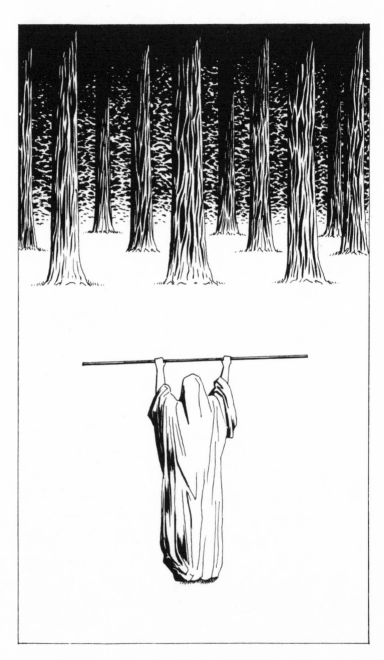

There they raised their arms, held their staff high,
and gave the ritual appeal for sufferance from the woods.

Korik suppressed the tonal lilt of his native tongue to speak the language of the Lords flatly, so that what he said was both a decision and a promise. 'We will pass through.'

With a silent nod, his comrades turned and called to the grazing Ranyhyn. Soon the company was mounted in formation, facing the Forest. Korik spoke quietly to Brabha, and the Ranyhyn started forward, walking directly at the fortifying brambles. When Brabha was close enough to nose the thorns, a narrow slit of path became visible before him.

In single file, the company walked into the shadowed demesne of Grimmerdhore.

The thorns plucked at them as they passed, but the Ranyhyn negotiated the path with such easy skill that even the long blue robes of the Lords suffered only small rents and snags. Yet the way was long and twisted, and Korik's senses quivered at the vulnerability of the company. If the brambles within the Forest were active, the riders were in grave danger. Korik sent a warning to the Bloodguard who rode nearest the Lords, and they braced themselves to jump to Hyrim's and Shetra's defence.

But none of the bushes moved: the low breeze carried no sound of awareness through the thorns. And then the brambles began to shrink and thin until they fell away like a sigh, leaving the riders in the hands of the Forest itself.

The air around them was thick and deep, almost audibly underlined with slumber; and it shifted faintly through the dim, mottled shadows like an uneasy rest, disturbed by dreams of damage and bloody repayment. It smelled so heavily of moss and damp mouldering soil and rot and growth that it was hard to breathe: it seemed to resist the lungs of the riders. And the crowded branches blocked out most of the sunlight: between occasional bright swathes of filtered lumination the trees seemed to brood in gloom, contemplating death.

But the quiet of Grimmerdhore was not as impenetrable as it had first appeared. From time to time, strange hoarse birds screeched forlornly. Black squirrels raced overhead. And frequently the Bloodguard heard frightened animals scuttling away from the company through the underbrush.

Still, the way became easier. The woods spread out within the perimeter of the brambles: the path broadened as if the trees were guarding it less closely; and animal trails wove back and forth around it. As a result, the company was able to resume its formation, with the Lords and Korik riding on the path and the other Bloodguard moving through the trees around them. Here the Ranyhyn went more quickly, almost at a trot; and the company moved straight in towards the heart of Grimmerdhore.

They rode as if they were passing through a reverie – the shaded and sombre musings of the Forest – until after dark. Except for Lord Hyrim's groans whenever he caught his balance, they travelled in silence, warding against something in the woods which might hear them. And even when he groaned, Hyrim gave no sign that he wished to stop or rest. He was caught up in Grimmerdhore's mood. But Korik

[65]

finally halted the company. The darkest facets of the night seemed to flourish under the trees; and though the Ranyhyn were still able to make their way, the Bloodguard could not see well enough to avoid any ambush which might lie ahead. Yet he felt an odd reluctance when he gave the command to settle the company for the night in a small open glade. He did not like to remain at the mercy of the Forest.

In Grimmerdhore the night was proof against the swarms of fireflies that hovered and darted through the woods. They blinked and danced like beacons for the myriad denizens of the dark – they flew around in a brave enchanting display – but they were effectless, made nothing else visible. When the Lords went to sleep on a flat mossy rock, and the Bloodguard spread out over the glade to stand watch, their security was marred by the fireflies. Those lights stiffened the darkness, walled it up. They drew the attention of the Bloodguard, and so helped to conceal everything else. At last, Korik and his comrades were forced to watch with their eyes closed – to rely on hearing, and smell, and the touch of the ground under their bare feet.

The next morning at the first night-thinning of dawn they resumed their progress. At first, Lord Hyrim was inclined to talk, as if he wished to dispel the enshrouding gloom. For a pretext, he took his horsemanship: he claimed in defiance of his obvious difficulties that it had improved. On that and related subjects he rambled through the dawn as if the rest of the company were listening to him spellbound. But gradually his speech became frayed like his robe, and as the sun rose he faltered into silence. Despite the sunlight, Grimmerdhore's mood was darkening around them; and he could no longer pretend he did not feel it.

As they approached the heart of the Forest, they were drawing closer to the source of Grimmerdhore's inarticulate ire.

By noon, the mood of the Forest dominated everything. Even the familiar creatures of the woods had fallen into a silence of their own: no bird-calls, no chattering or scurrying, no noise of life lifted itself up against the prevailing dumb passion of the trees. Instead, something new came into the air – something musky and mephitic. It irritated Korik's nostrils like the smell of burning blood, made him want to jerk his head aside as if to avoid a blow. Lord Shetra barked softly, 'Wolves!' and he knew that she was right. Their spoor hung in the air as if there were a great pack running just ahead of the Ranyhyn.

The smell troubled Brabha. He shook his mane, shorted angrily. But when Korik asked the old Ranyhyn if the wolves were nearby, Brabha indicated with a toss of his head that they were not. Then Korik urged the company ahead until it was moving as fast as Lord Hyrim's inept seat permitted.

Throughout the afternoon, they thrust constantly deeper into Grimmerdhore's distress. After a time, the reek of the wolves stopped growing, and as a result it lost some of its immediacy. But the mood of the trees suffered no such diminution. Rather, the company seemed to be riding into a deepening sea of emotion. Though the lingering consciousness of

Grimmerdhore had been reduced to hebetude by time and the ancient slaughter of the One Forest, it was slowly taking heat, mounting toward outrage. In the evening, the breeze stiffened, lifted up the murmurous language of the trees and gave it a tone of execration – as if Grimmerdhore were struggling against slumber, against the inflexibility of wood and the chains of old time, to utter a root-deep hatred. When the riders stopped for the night, the darkness, and the smell of the wolves, and the strangled howl of the trees clung to them. And there were no fireflies.

Korik gauged that they were halfway through the Forest.

'But all in all,' Lord Hyrim said in a tone of hollow cheer, 'we have been fortunate. Grimmerdhore is dismayed in good sooth. Yet it is in my heart that this dismay is not the pain of the Despiser's presence. It is not his armies which lie before us, but rather some other instance of his malice.'

'And by that we are made fortunate?' Shetra asked tightly.

'Of a surety.' Hyrim tried to summon his wonted playfulness; but his tone failed. 'We are but two Lords and fifteen Bloodguard. Against an army we are doomed. But perhaps we will suffice to flee this smaller ill.'

In response, the stiff Lord glowered at him without speaking; but her heart was elsewhere.

She and Hyrim lay down, attempted to sleep. But the mood of the Forest grew, seemed now to gain virulence with each passing moment. Both Lords had given up rest and were on their feet staring into the dark with the Bloodguard when the first glimmer of light appeared north of them.

As they watched it, transfixed, the light became stronger and sharper, spread a hot orange glow through the trees. And with every brighter surge of glow, the Forest increased its silent cry of horror, outrage.

'Fire!' Lord Shetra gritted fiercely. 'By the Seven! A fire has been set. In Grimmerdhore!'

– Call the Ranyhyn, Korik commanded. Strike camp. Take formation. We must shun this peril.

Gasping, *'Melenkurion abatha!'* Lord Hyrim ran toward his mount. An instinctive energy possessed him, and he struggled without help onto the back of the Ranyhyn. Clutching his staff, knotting his other hand in the mane of the horse, he turned toward the fire.

Lord Shetra followed him in an instant. She vaulted onto her Ranyhyn, sprang forward, plunged through the underbrush after Hyrim.

– Halt them! Korik shouted. I will have no more Kevins. The mission must not fail!

He leaped astride Brabha and galloped after the Lords. But he saw through the firelit woods that he would not catch them in time. Shetra rode well; and the Ranyhyn bearing Hyrim displayed fine skill by keeping him in his seat.

Korik shouted after them, commanding them to stop with all the metal of his personal strength.

Lord Hyrim made no response. He crashed through the woods as if he were oblivious to caution. But Lord Shetra wheeled her Ranyhyn once. Immediately, Korik reached her side. Sill and Runnik flashed past in pursuit of Hyrim.

'The mission is in our hands,' Korik snapped to Shetra. 'We must flee this peril.'

'And let Grimmerdhore burn?' she almost shrieked. 'We would cease to be Lords!'

Slapping the Ranyhyn with her heels, she raced after Hyrim and his pursuers.

Korik followed her with the other Bloodguard. He demanded the best speed Brabha could manage through the trees. Ahead of him, Lord Hyrim crested the hill and dropped out of sight, dashing straight into the glow of the fire. But he was no longer alone. Sill had joined him, and Runnik was only one stride behind.

Moments later, Korik topped the hill with Shetra, Cerrin, and the other Bloodguard galloping beside him. Before them was a wide, almost treeless valley shaped like a bowl. The fire raged in its bottom. And around the conflagration capered a score of black forms.

Ur-viles.

They were burning a huge Gilden.

As the company charged down the hillside, Korik could hear the surrounding Forest's choked effort to scream.

He bent low over Brabha's neck, urged the Ranyhyn faster. Ahead, he picked out the loremaster of the ur-viles. It whirled its tapering iron stave and slapped power in a black liquid at the tree. At each new burst of fire, it slavered gleefully. But when it saw the approaching company, it barked a command at the other ur-viles. The whole group dropped its rapacious dance and sprinted away to the north.

Lord Hyrim ignored them. He went right to the fire, tumbled from the back of his mount. When he hit the ground, he fell, then rolled and bounced up again. Standing almost in the blaze, he held his staff over his head with both hands and began shouting words of power.

The next moment, Shetra rushed past him after the fleeing ur-viles. Like an angry hawk, she swooped across the bottom of the valley and started up the northern slope. Korik and the other Bloodguard hurried behind her as she closed on her prey.

Before the Ur-Viles could react,
Korik sprang from Brabha's back.

At a sharp call from the loremaster, the ur-viles turned to fight. Instantly, they formed their close fighting wedge, with the loremaster at the point. In this formation, they could focus all their combined power through the lore-master's stave. As Lord Shetra attacked, the wedge lashed out at her. Her Ranyhyn jumped aside to avoid the loremaster's black thrust; and momentum carried her past the wedge.

Before the ur-viles could react, Korik sprang from Brabha's back. He dove over the loremaster, crashed like a battering-ram into the centre of the wedge. Pren, Tull, and three more Bloodguard followed him; and their force scattered the ur-viles, breaking the concentration of the wedge.

But these attacks still left the loremaster untouched. While Shetra wheeled back to the battle, the loremaster threw power into the air with its stave and gave a raw barking cry like a signal. As he fought, Korik looked about him for hidden enemies.

Then Lord Shetra charged again. Holding her staff by one end, she chopped savagely at the loremaster. It caught her blow with its stave; but without the wedge behind it, it could not match her. With a hot blue burst of force, her staff split the iron stave. The loremaster fell, crushed by the backlash of the concussion.

During the blast, Korik received an urgent call from Sill. He completed his last blow, then left the remaining ur-viles to the abundant strength of his comrades and spun away to look around the valley.

Down at the bottom of the bowl, Lord Hyrim was laboring strenuously to save the Gilden. In a voice shrill with strain, he summoned the Earthpower to his aid. And he was making progress. In answer to his invocations, water bubbled up from the grass around the tree – already it was deep enough to touch his ankles – and the fire gradually sloughed away from the broad limbs, dropped down as if the tree were shrugging off of cloak of flame.

Still, the process was hard, slow. Hyrim sounded exhausted, and he had not subdued a quarter of the blaze.

But that was not the meaning of Sill's

shout. After one brief glance at Hyrim, Korik saw the other peril.

There were wolves standing shoulder to shoulder around the entire rim of the valley.

They were poised and silent, gazing intently down into the bowl: their eyes reflected the fire, so that the valley seemed ringed by a thousand red pairs of waiting fireflies. But even as Korik scanned them, took a rough estimate of their numbers, the leader of the pack threw back its head and gave a long high yipping howl.

Brabha returned a furious neigh, as if he were answering a challenge.

It affected the wolves like a tantara. At once, they broke into a hungry growl that pulsed in the air like the turmoil of seas. And they started down into the valley at a slow walk.

– A trap, Cerrin said. We have been snared.

Korik called to Lord Shetra, then bounded onto Brabha's back and pelted down the hillside toward the tree. The rest of the company followed him instantly. As he reached the fire, he ordered the Bloodguard into a defensive formation around him. To Lord Hyrim, he shouted, 'Come!'

Hyrim did not turn his head. With sweat running down his cheeks and a wide intensity like obsession in his eyes, he kept working for the tree: he invoked water as if he were heaving it out of the ground by main force of will, vitalized the tree's resistance to flame, and now pulled at the fire itself, drawing it slowly tongue by tongue, away from the branches. But through the slow beats of the *lillianrill* chant he wove for the Gilden, he hissed to Korik, 'It must be saved!'

– This task consumes him, Sill said. He urges the mission to go without him.

– He will be slain, Korik snapped.

– Not while I live.

– You will not live long.

– That is the way with him, Sill shrugged silently.

Korik had no time to debate whether or not he should desert one Lord for the sake of the mission. He did not intend to make that choice.

Summon or succour. Swiftly, he threw himself from Brabha, stepped in front of Hyrim. He could not allow the son of Hoole to commit suicide. Almost wincing at the way he was forced to violate his Vowed service to any Lord, he shouted into Hyrim's concentration, 'Will you sacrifice the Giants for one tree?'

The Lord did not stop. His eyes reflected the fire with a ferocity Korik had never seen in him before. He seemed to be sweating passion as he panted, 'The choice is not so simple!'

Korik reached our a hand to wrest Hyrim away from his mad purpose. But at that instant Shetra barked, 'Korik, you forget yourself!' and cast her power like a shout to Hyrim's support. The sheer force of their combined exertion made Korik recoil a step.

The wolves were almost upon them: the bristling growl filled the air with the sound of fangs.

Briskly, Korik marshalled his comrades around him on their mounts. The Ranyhyn champed and snorted tensely, but held their positions against the slow advance of the wolves.

Together, the Lords gave a wild cry; and the light of Gilden-fire fell suddenly out of the night.

As darkness rushed back into the valley, Hyrim stumbled against Korik, nearly fell. Korik half threw the Lord to Sill, who boosted Hyrim up onto his mount.

Shouting the company into motion, Korik leaped for Brabha's back.

The next moment, the leading wolves attacked. But with a heave of their mighty muscles, the Ranyhyn started together toward the east. In close formation, they struck the springing wall of the wolves – and the wall broke like a wave on a jutting fist of rock. The Ranyhyn surged through the pack, shedding wolves like water, striving to gain speed. At first their head-on charge threw the pack into confusion. But then the wolves chasing them came close enough to leap onto their backs. Pren and four other Bloodguard in the rear of the company were about to be engulfed.

Lord Shetra slowed her mount. Reacting instinctively, the Bloodguard parted behind her, let her drop back beside Pren. As the flood of wolves came toward her, she swung her staff at them. The blow knocked down the first beasts and set flame to them, so that they flared up like tinder. The following pack jumped aside from the sudden fire: the rush was momentarily broken.

In that respite, the Ranyhyn reached full stride. Plunging to keep away from the fangs, they laboured up the slope. The pack raged at their heels; but they were Ranyhyn, swifter even than the yellow *kresh*. By the time they topped the valley's rim and thundered back into the closed woods, they were three strides ahead of the pack.

Then through the depths of Grimmerdhore the Ranyhyn raced the wolves. Korik could no longer see as well as the horses, so he abandoned to them all concern for the direction and safety of the run. Unchecked, they dodged deftly through the night as if they were riding the wind. But still the Forest hampered them, interfered with their running, prevented them from their best speed. And the wolves were not hampered. They swept along the ground easily, passed through the woods like a black tide. When they gave tongue to the chase, they did not break stride.

The gap between the pack and the company shrank and grew as Grimmerdhore thickened and thinned. Through one tight copse Pren and his clan-kin had to fend off wolves on both sides. But fortunately the terrain beyond was relatively open; and the Ranyhyn were able to restore the gap.

During it all – the dodging, the surging pace, the unevenness of the ground – Lord Hyrim clung to his seat. He was kept there by the proud skill of his mount. And the other Ranyhyn aided him by choosing their ways so that his horse had the straightest path through the trees. When he observed this, Korik applauded silently, and his chest grew tight with admiration, in spite of the other demands on his attention.

Still the race went on. The Ranyhyn

pounded through the Forest with growing abandon, discounting the safety of the company more and more for the sake of speed. As a result the riders had to hold their seats when they were lashed by branches, wrenched from side to side while the horses evaded looming trunks. But the savage pursuit of the wolves did not abate. Clearly, the will which drove them was strong and compelling; and Korik guessed that a powerful band of ur-viles remained in Grimmerdhore – a force which used the wolves just as it had used the Gilden and the other ur-viles. But such thoughts were of no value now. The wolves were the immediate danger. Hundreds of ravenous throats howled: hundreds of jaws gaped and bit furiously, as if they were too eager to wait for the raw flesh of the company. The Ranyhyn gave their best speed – and the pack did not fall behind.

Korik was revolving desperate solutions in his mind when the company broke out into a broad open glade. Under the stars, he saw the ravine which cut through the centre of the glade across the company's path. It was an old dry

The Ranyhyn leap the gorge.

watercourse, deeply eroded before its source turned elsewhere. And it was far too wide for the wolves: they could not leap it. If the Ranyhyn could manage the jump, the company would gain precious time.

But when the wolves burst out of the woods, they broke into hard howls of triumph. In a few strides, Korik saw his danger: the ravine appeared to be too wide even for the Ranyhyn. For an instant, he hesitated. In his long years, he had heard the shrieking of horses far too often. He knew how the Ranyhyn would scream if they shattered their bones against the opposite wall of the ravine. But their night-sight was better than his: he could not make this decision for them. He silenced his fears, shouted to his comrades:

– Let the Ranyhyn choose! They will not err! But ward Lord Hyrim!

Then Runnik reached the ravine. His mount gathered itself, seemed for an instant to shrink, to coil in on its strength – and sprang. Already it was too late for the rest of the riders to stop; but Korik kept his eyes on Runnik,

[85]

watched the leading Ranyhyn so that he would have an instant's warning of his fate – an instant in which to try to save himself for the sake of the mission. For the first time since the night when he had assumed his Vow, he left the Lords to their own fortunes. He expected Hyrim to fall. As old Brabha started into his own jump, the Lord wailed as if he were plunging from a precipice.

Then the Ranyhyn carrying Runnik touched down safely on the far side of the ravine. Beside him, Tull and another Bloodguard also landed with ground to spare, followed by Cerrin, Shetra, Korik, Hyrim, and Sill in a line together. Lord Hyrim flopped forward and back as if his mount were bucking: his wail was broken off. But he did not lose his seat. Amid the wild yowling frustration of the wolves, the rest of the Bloodguard jumped the ravine. The Ranyhyn sprinted across the glade with clear ground at their heels.

Behind them, the wolves rushed on, caught in the grip of a dementing passion. They piled into the dry watercourse, careless of what happened to them, and scrambled furiously up the far side. But Korik was confident of escape now. The company had almost reached the edge of the glade when the first wolf clawed its way out of the ravine. Korik leaned forward to say a word of praise in Brabha's back-bent ears.

Out of the corner of his eye, he saw Lord Hyrim tumble like a lifeless sack to the ground.

Korik shouted to the company. Immediately, the leaders peeled around to return to Hyrim as fast as possible. But Pren, the rearmost Bloodguard, saw Hyrim's fall in time to leap down from his own mount. In a few steps, he reached the motionless Lord. While Korik and the others were turning, Pren reported that Hyrim was unconscious – stunned either by his fall or by the jolt of the jump over the ravine.

Wheeling Brabha, Korik gauged the distances. The wolves surged out of the ravine in great numbers now: they howled rabidly toward the men on the ground. The company would barely have time to snatch up Hyrim and take defensive positions around him before the pack struck.

But as Korik pulled his comrades into formation, Lord Shetra ordered him back. She had a plan of her own. Driving her mount straight for Hyrim, she called to Pren, 'His staff! Hold it upright!'

Pren obeyed swiftly. He caught up Hyrim's staff from the grass, gripped it with one metal-shod end planted on the ground between him and the charging wolves.

As he did this, Shetra swung her Ranyhyn until she was running parallel to the line of the charge. When she flashed behind Pren, she cried, *'Melenkurion abatha!'* and dealt Hyrim's staff a hammering blow with her own.

A silent concussion shook the air: the ground seemed to heave momentarily under the hooves of the Ranyhyn. From Hyrim's staff a plane of power spread out on both sides, came like a wall between the wolves and the company across the whole eastern face of the glade. Seen through this barrier, the scrambling wolves appeared distorted, mad, wronged.

Then they smashed into the wall. In that instant, the area of impact flared like a sheet of blue lightning; and the wolves were thrown back. They charged it again as more of them reached it, hurled themselves against the rippling plane – howled and raved, assaulted the air. But wherever they hit the wall, it flared blue and cast them back. Soon they were crashing into it in such numbers that the whole plane across the length of the glade caught fire. Where the greatest weight of the pack pressed and fought against it, it scaled upward into dazzling brightness. Carefully, Shetra withdrew Hyrim's staff from the plane. It wavered as if it were about to break; but she sang to it softly, and it steadied, stood up firmly under the strain.

It was too much for the wolves. In a wild excess of passion and frustration, they began to attack each other – venting their driven rage on the nearest flesh until the whole place was consumed in a boiling melee.

Lord Shetra turned away as if the sight hurt her. She appeared suddenly weary: the

He caught up Hyrim's staff from the grass.

exertion of commanding two staffs had drained her. Dully, she said to Korik, 'We must go. If it is assailed again, my Word will not endure. And if there are ur-viles nearby, they will know how to counter it. I am too worn to speak another.' Then she knelt to examine Hyrim.

In a moment, she ascertained that he had no broken bones, no internal bleeding, no concussion. She left him to Korik and Sill. Working rapidly, they placed Hyrim on the back of his Ranyhyn and lashed him there with *clingor* thongs. When he was secured, the Bloodguard sprang to their own mounts, and the company hurried away into the covered darkness of Grimmerdhore.

The Ranyhyn moved at a near gallop. Soon the intervening Forest quenched the tumult of the wolves, and the company was surrounded by a welcome silence. But still they ran: they did not stop or slow, even when Lord Hyrim returned to groaning consciousness. They left him alone until he was alert enough to free himself from the *clingor*. Then Lord Shetra explained to him shortly, in a tired voice, what had happened.

He took the news dumbly, nodded his comprehension of her words. Then he lay down on the Ranyhyn's neck as if he were hiding his head and clung there through the rest of the night.

At dawn, Korik called a halt beside a stream to water the horses and allow the Lords to eat a few treasure-berries. But after that they moved on again at a fast canter. Korik did not want to spend another night in Grimmerdhore; and he could feel Brabha's eagerness to break out of the dark woods.

The fatigue, the lack of rest, the unrelieved haste of their journey showed in both Lords: Hyrim's eyes, formerly so gay, had a grey angle of pain; and Shetra's lean face was lined and sharpened, as if some erosion had cut away the last softness of her features. But they endured. As time passed, they found deeper springs of strength to sustain them.

Korik should have been reassured. But he was not. The Lords had proven themselves

Korik Bloodguard

equal to wolves and Grimmerdhore. But he had reason to know that what lay ahead would be worse.